The Upstairs Cat

by **Karla Kuskin** ~ Illustrated by **Howard Fine**

Clarion Books ~ *New York*

Clarion Books
a Houghton Mifflin Company imprint
215 Park Avenue South, New York, NY 10003
Text copyright © 1997 by Karla Kuskin
Illustrations copyright © 1997 by Howard Fine

The illustrations for this book were executed in pastel.
The text is set in 20/25-point Horley Oldstyle.

For information about this and other Houghton Mifflin trade and reference books
and multimedia products, visit The Bookstore at Houghton Mifflin on the
World Wide Web at (http://www.hmco.com/trade/).

Printed in the USA

Library of Congress Cataloging-in-Publication Data
Kuskin, Karla.
    The upstairs cat / by Karla Kuskin ; illustrated by Howard Fine.
    p.   cm.
    Summary: The fights between a mean, old cat and a lean, young cat always end
in a draw and result in a waste of energy which proves the futility of war.
    ISBN 0-395-70146-5
    [1. Cats—Fiction. 2. Fighting (Psychology)—Fiction.   3. War—
Fiction.   4. Stories in rhyme.] I. Fine, Howard, ill. II. Title.
PZ8.3.K96Up   1997
[E]—dc20   95-50523
CIP
AC

HOR   10 9 8 7 6 5 4 3 2 1

For Amelia Jane Kuskin, who was born in July.
—*K. K.*

For Olivia and Nathaniel.
—*H. F*

Let's begin with the facts.
The facts are that
there's an upstairs cat
and a downstairs cat.

One older and meaner,
one younger and leaner,
engaged in a war
that neither is winning.

That is the beginning.

The fighting continues
to never quite stop,
one cat at the bottom
and one at the top
of the stairs in between,
with their stares in between,
if you see what I mean.

They sit and they stare.
Well, they glare at each other.
Then one dares a stair
and one dares the other.

And suddenly there is a mad confrontation,
the kind that blows up
on the border of nations.

Skirmishing,
growling,
the yowls of a riot,
until a voice yells
"*CUT THAT OUT.*"

Then there's quiet.

And younger and leaner,
quite proud in demeanor
but secretly scared,

tiptoes downstairs
and curls in a chair.

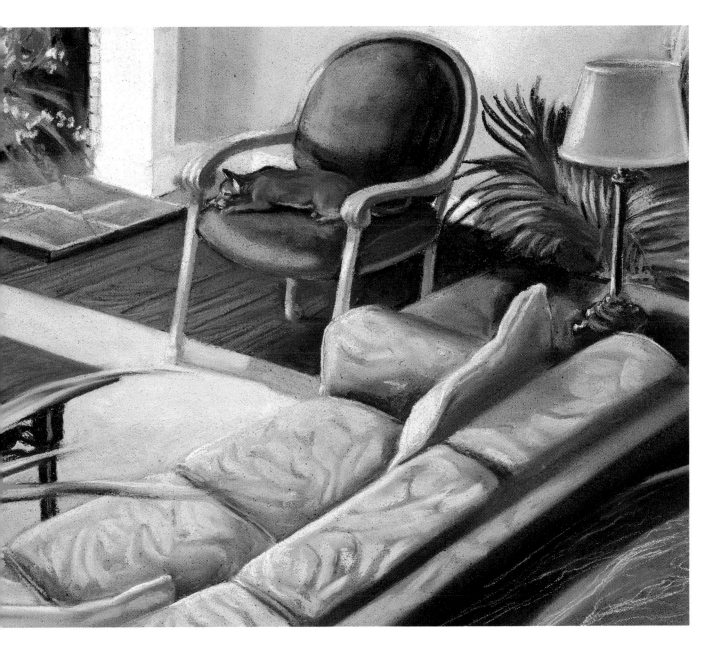

While upstairs
the older,
who only *looks* meaner,
mutters bad things
about younger and leaner.

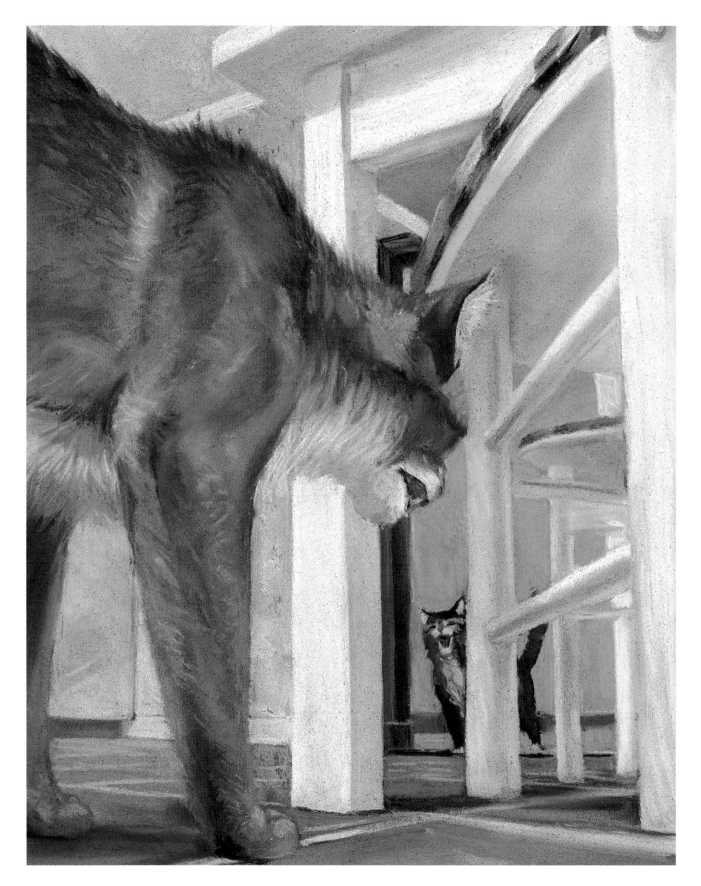

Now each is a good cat,
the two *could* be friends.
Instead they are enemies.
That's where it ends.

Except, as I said
at the start of this rhyme,
their fighting repeats itself

time after time

after week after month

after year after year.

And nothing is dumber
than war.

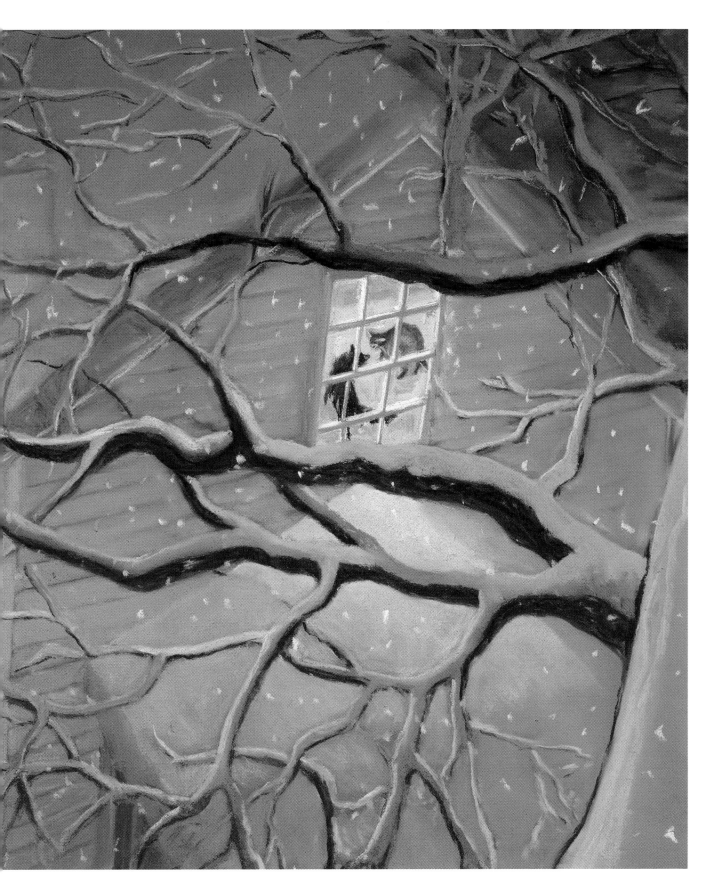

Is that clear?